The Tiara Club
at Diamond Turrets

For Princess Joy,
(and her magical aunt S as well).
Much love, Viv xxxx

With very special thanks to JD

www.tiaraclub.co.uk

ORCHARD BOOKS
338 Euston Road, London NW1 3BH
Orchard Books Australia
Level 17/207 Kent St, Sydney, NSW 2000

A Paperback Original
First published in Great Britain in 2009
Text © Vivian French 2009
Cover illustration © Sarah Gibb 2009
Inside illustrations © Orchard Books 2009

A CIP catalogue record for this book is available
from the British Library.

ISBN 978 1 84616 877 2

1 3 5 7 9 10 8 6 4 2

Printed in Great Britain

Orchard Books is a division of Hachette Children's Books,
an Hachette UK company
www.hachette.co.uk

The Tiara Club
at Diamond Turrets

Princess Caitlin
and the Little Lamb

By Vivian French

ORCHARD BOOKS

The Royal Palace Academy
for the Preparation of Perfect Princesses

(Known to our students as "*The Princess Academy*")

OUR SCHOOL MOTTO:
A Perfect Princess always thinks of others
before herself, and is kind, caring and truthful.

Diamond Turrets offers a complete education for
Tiara Club princesses, focusing on caring for animals
and the environment. The curriculum includes:

A visit to the Royal
County Show

Visits to the Country
Park and Bamboo Grove

Work experience on our
very own farm

Elephant rides in our
Safari Park (students
will be closely supervised)

Our headteacher, King Percy, is present at all times, and
students are well looked after by Fairy G, the school
Fairy Godmother.

Our resident staff and visiting experts include:

LADY WHITSTABLE-KENT
(IN CHARGE OF THE FARM,
COUNTRY PARK AND SAFARI PARK)

QUEEN MOTHER MATILDA
(ETIQUETTE, POSTURE AND
APPEARANCE)

FAIRY ANGORA
(ASSISTANT FAIRY GODMOTHER)

FARMER KATE
(DOMESTIC ANIMALS)

LADY MAY (SUPERVISOR OF THE
HOLIDAY HOME FOR PETS)

We award tiara points to encourage our Tiara Club princesses towards the next level. All princesses who win enough points at Diamond Turrets will be presented with their Diamond Sashes and attend a celebration ball.

Diamond Sash Tiara Club princesses are invited to return to Golden Gates, our magnificent mansion residence for Perfect Princesses, where they may continue their education at a higher level.

PLEASE NOTE:
Princesses are expected to arrive at
the Academy with a *minimum* of:

TWENTY BALLGOWNS
(with all necessary hoops,
petticoats, etc)

DANCING SHOES
five pairs

TWELVE DAY DRESSES

VELVET SLIPPERS
three pairs

SEVEN GOWNS
suitable for garden parties
and other special
day occasions

RIDING BOOTS
two pairs

Wellington boots, waterproof
cloaks and other essential
protective clothing
as required

TWELVE TIARAS

Hello! How are you *doing*?
I'm *Princess Caitlin*, and I'm
very, VERY pleased to meet you!
Have you met the rest of Tulip Room
here at Diamond Turrets? There's
Amelia, and Bethany, Lindsey, Abigail and
Rebecca - and me and you, of course.
It's wonderful here, even though
the twins, Diamonde and Gruella,
are always causing trouble...

Chapter One

The Royal County Show

I thought Lindsey was going to burst with excitement when she came zooming into the recreation room. It was just before bedtime, and she'd been to look at the school notice board to see if we had an extra art lesson the next day. Mia thought we did, but I was sure we didn't.

Anyway, Lindsey came whizzing back, her cheeks bright pink and her eyes sparkling. She very nearly ran Diamonde over, and of course Diamonde screeched – but for once Lindsey didn't stop to apologise.

"LOOK!" she said, and she waved a piece of paper under our noses. "It's a competition, and the winner gets to lead a little orphan lamb in the Grand Procession at the Royal County Show!"

We all practically smothered Lindsey as we tried to see the paper at once, and she burst out laughing.

"I'll read it to you," she said. "'All princesses are invited to create a costume suitable for farm work. You may work individually, in pairs, or in a group of not more than six. Consideration must be given to comfort and practicality before elegance. Princesses will be expected to wear their costumes on the day of the Royal County Show. There will be a formal parade at ten o'clock, and the entries will be judged by Her

Most Gracious Majesty Queen Frizella Marie—'"

"WHAT'S THAT?" Diamonde absolutely GRABBED the paper out of Lindsey's hand.

"Just wait a minute!" I said indignantly, staring at Diamonde. "Lindsey was reading that!"

Diamonde gave me a snooty stare back. "Actually, Caitlin, Queen Frizella Marie is our great aunt, so we know who'll win, don't we, Gruella?"

Gruella looked very surprised. "Do we?"

Diamonde gave a heavy sigh. "US, of course!"

"But Queen Frizella Marie isn't the only judge," Lindsey pointed out. "There are three names on the list."

Diamonde frowned, and looked down at the paper again. "Lady Whitstable-Kent, King Percy and Queen Frizella Marie. The school farm manager, our headteacher, and the most important queen for miles and miles and MILES around. Hmm. Well, we know who's the most important of those three, don't we, Gruella?"

"Oh, yes," Gruella simpered. "King Percy. He's SO handsome."

Diamonde went bright purple.

"Honestly, Gruella," she snapped, "sometimes you don't see what's under your nose. WE are going to win, because Queen Frizella Marie is sure to choose us. Come on! Let's go and design our winning costume!" And she seized her twin's arm, bundling her out of the recreation room.

"Goodness," Rebecca said as the door slammed shut behind them. "Do you think she's right?"

Mia laughed. "No," she said. "King Percy would never have asked anyone to judge the competition who wasn't going to be fair."

Abigail grinned. "'A Perfect Princess is always fair whatever the circumstances'," she quoted, and pulled her drawing book out of her bag. "Shall we have a go at some designs?"

"Good idea," I said, and I hunted around for a pencil. The only one I had was broken, but luckily Bethany had loads of colouring pencils.

"What kind of thing should we choose?" Lindsey asked.

"Let's see." Abigail looked thoughtful. "Something pretty but practical, I'd say."

I twirled a crayon. "Not like Little Bo Peep, then—" and I leant over Abigail's shoulder and drew a girl with a wide hooped dress and an old-fashioned sun bonnet.

"That's really good!" Abigail told me, and she gave the girl

VERY high heeled shoes.

"Oh! Do let me have a go!" Lindsey begged, and she added a crook. Then Rebecca drew a bow on it, and Mia coloured the dress pale green.

Bethany began to giggle, and she wrote:

1. Green dress so it won't show grass stains.

2. Lots of frilly petticoats to keep Perfect Princesses warm when it's cold.

3. High heels for peering over hedges.

4. Sun bonnet to protect Perfect Princesses' noses.

5. Crook for catching runaway lambs.

6. Ribbon to tie round the lamb's neck.

"I've thought of something else," Abigail said, and she added...

7. Lovely smile in case a handsome prince comes walking by...

That made us all laugh.

"Wouldn't it be DREADFUL if we had to dress like that?" I said. "Can you imagine trying to feed the pigs wearing frilly petticoats?"

"Terrible," Bethany agreed.

The school bell rang for bedtime, and Rebecca sighed. "We'd better go up to Tulip Room," she said, and we hurried off, leaving our silly drawing on the table.

Chapter Two

Halfway along the corridor we met the twins going in the other direction. Gruella said hello, but Diamonde stuck her nose in the air and pretended we weren't there.

"Where are they off to?" Abigail wondered. "Their room's the same side of the building as ours."

"Who knows," Bethany said.

"Maybe they left something in the recreation room."

"Oh!" I stopped dead. "We have too! We've left our Little Bo Peep drawing, and I REALLY wanted to show Rose Room!"

"I'll go and fetch it," Lindsey said, and she rolled away at speed. The rest of us walked on to Tulip Room, and began to get ready for bed.

Have I told you about our room? It's SO pretty – every time I go in it I feel happy. There are tulips absolutely everywhere; even our pillows have the sweetest little tulips embroidered in the corner.

I'm SO glad I'm here, rather than in Rose or Daffodil or Lily Room; tulips are definitely my most favourite flower.

We'd just finished cleaning our teeth when Lindsey came back. She was looking disappointed, and she said she couldn't find our picture anywhere.

"That's weird," Rebecca said. "I'm sure we left it on the table."

"Maybe the cleaners threw it away," Bethany suggested.

Lindsey nodded. "I met Fairy Angora on my way back, and she said the same. Oh, and she said there IS an extra art class tomorrow – all morning! We can use it to draw our real designs for the competition, she said, and she'll help us."

We looked at each other in delight. Fairy Angora is the school's assistant fairy godmother, and everybody loves her to bits. We were going to have the most FABULOUS time!

*

Have you noticed that whenever you think something's going to be AMAZING it often goes all wrong? Fairy Angora didn't take our art lesson after all. She sent a message to say she had to go to

a meeting, and Queen Mother Matilda took it instead, and she's SO different. When Mia drew a lovely picture of a princess wearing jodhpurs, and Rebecca added a cute little jacket, Queen Mum Mattie actually sniffed.

"HARDLY the outfit for a Perfect Princess," she remarked, and swept away to where the twins were. "Now THIS," she said, "is SO much nicer! Take five tiara points each!" We didn't see what the twins had drawn, though. They kept their arms curled round their picture as if they were scared someone would steal their idea.

In the end we decided to go for the jodhpurs and jacket, with a pretty short-sleeved blouse in case the weather got hot. We thought that would be OK for all kinds of farm work.

"Why don't we embroider some flowers on the jacket to make it prettier?" Bethany suggested.

I clapped my hands. "Of course! Let's have tulips!"

"Lovely pink ones," Abigail said quickly, and we all agreed.

"What happens now?" Rebecca asked. "Do we have to make them ourselves?"

I put my hand up and asked Queen Mother Matilda, and she gave me a chilly look. "In MY day," she said, "a Perfect Princess would NEVER be expected to actually WORK with animals. And here you all are designing an outfit for it! You'll have to check with Lady Whitstable-Kent. I understand that she and King Percy dreamt up this competition.'

"Oh." I wasn't quite sure what to say. "So shall I go and ask Lady Whit, Your Majesty?"

Queen Mother Matilda nodded. "Be as quick as you can."

I curtsied, and hurried out of the art room. I thought Lady Whit would be in her office, but I met her in the corridor looking flustered.

"Ah! Princess Caitlin! Could you run down to the farm with a message for Farmer Kate? Tell her we'll need the lamb to be in the Royal Marquee at ten o'clock, not eleven."

"Of course," I said, but I didn't go straight away. "Erm...will it be all right, though? Queen Mother Matilda said I was to hurry back as soon as I'd asked you how our outfits are to be made."

"Oh – Fairy G's seeing to all that." Lady Whit waved her arm dismissively. "She'll be in the sewing room all afternoon. And tell Queen Mother Matilda you were running an errand for me."

"Thank you very much," I said, and I skipped happily out into the sunshine.

Chapter Three

It took me no time to run down to the farm buildings, and I found Farmer Kate in the yard. When I gave her Lady Whit's message she said, "No problem. I'll have Topper there for ten. Would you like to meet him?"

I followed her to one of the sheds and there, nestled in the straw, was the SWEETEST lamb. He had a snow-white coat with three black spots on his back, and as soon as he saw Kate he bounced towards her.

Kate looked at me. "Why don't you give him his bottle?" she asked, and I nearly fell over with excitement. "Yes, PLEASE," I said.

Have you ever fed a baby lamb? It's SUCH fun! Topper sucked and sucked until every single drop was gone, and then he let me scratch his ears while he wriggled with pleasure. "You've done well," Kate said. "He really likes you."

"I'll see him in the Grand Parade," I said, and I ran back to school. I was so busy thinking about Topper that if I hadn't seen Lady Whit striding out of her office I might have forgotten to tell her that everything was all right. She thanked me, and I arrived back in the art room just as the bell went for lunch. I was bursting to talk to my friends, but as I came through the door I was met by a FURIOUS Queen Mother Matilda.

"Princess Caitlin!" She glared at me. "I don't know WHAT you've been doing, but you are LATE, and you are FILTHY! Take five minus tiara points! And I shall tell King Percy you do NOT deserve to take part in the competition!" And she swept away before I could say a single word.

*

I didn't talk much during lunch. My friends tried to cheer me up, and Lindsey even offered to go and tell Queen Mum Mattie it wasn't my fault, but I still felt miserable. Diamonde and Gruella were sitting at our table and they spent the whole time boasting about how they were SURE to win the competition, and that didn't make things any better.

"We're going to put pretty pale green ribbons on the little lamb," Gruella told us.

"You mean BLUE ribbons!" Diamonde snapped.

"But in that picture—" Gruella began, but she didn't finish. Diamonde piled up their plates with a crash, and swept her away.

"I think we should go to the sewing room early," Mia said, "so we can ask Fairy G if Caitlin's really been banned from the competition."

"Good thinking, Mia," Rebecca agreed, and we set off along the corridor. I was almost shaking as we walked through the sewing room door.

Our school fairy godmother was arranging material in piles, but when she saw me she smiled,

and I began to feel better.

"Aha!" she said, her eyes twinkling. "I hear you've been running away from lessons to play with little lambs!"

"If you please, Fairy G," I said, "I really, REALLY didn't mean to be so long."

Fairy G nodded. "It's quite all right. Lady Whit sorted it out at lunchtime. I'm afraid you've still got your minus tiara points, though. Queen Mother Matilda says that NO Perfect Princess walks round with straw in her hair! Now, have you got your design with you?"

Of course we had, and Mia produced it with a flourish.

"Good," Fairy G said. "Let's get busy!"

Chapter Five

It was SUCH fun! We chose a gorgeous green velvet for the jackets so the embroidered tulips would show up nicely, and the prettiest pink for the blouse. The jodhpurs were dark grey, and Rebecca asked if they could be easy to wash.

"Goodness," Fairy G said. "You

ARE practical! What about boots?"

"We'd like them made of rubber, so they'll be easy to clean as well," Lindsey explained.

Fairy G beamed, and waved her wand. At once sparkles floated in the air, and six pairs of the most ELEGANT rubber boots appeared from nowhere.

"Oooooh!" The twins were in

the doorway. "Look, Gruella! Caitlin's going to be in the competition after all!" Diamonde did NOT sound pleased.

"But she won't have a dress like mine, will she?" Gruella sounded anxious.

Diamonde inspected our green velvet. "No," she said, and then hesitated. "Have Tulip Room finished, Fairy G?"

"Very nearly," Fairy G told her. "You can choose your material while you're waiting."

"But we don't want them to see, do we, Diamonde?" Gruella nudged her sister.

Diamonde went pink. "Actually," she said quickly, "we'll come back later."

Fairy G raised her eyebrows, but she didn't say anything as they scurried out.

"Six and six and twenty-two – now let's see what we can do!" she boomed. With a wave of her wand she filled the sewing room with sparkling stars...and we saw six neat piles of clothes on the table in front of us!

The morning of the Royal County Show was cloudy, but we didn't mind. We were SO excited as we got dressed, and I know this sounds boastful, but we DID look amazing!

"Pretty AND practical," Lindsey said as we twirled in front of our mirror. "What time did Fairy G say the coaches were coming?"

"Half past nine," Mia said.

Abigail tweaked the collar of her jacket, and asked, "Has anyone seen what the horrible twins are wearing yet?"

Bethany shook her head. "No – but we'll find out when we go into the hall."

But we didn't. The twins still hadn't appeared when the coaches arrived, and Fairy Angora hurried us into the first one. "You look lovely, my little petals," she said as she climbed in with us. "Fairy G will come in the last coach, and we're all ready to cheer you on in the parade!"

*

I think we all had flutters in our stomachs as we arrived. The marquee where the parade was to be held was ENORMOUS!

Fairy Angora led us inside, and we saw King Percy and Lady Whit talking to a queen who looked VERY superior.

"That must be Queen Frizella Marie," Rebecca whispered in my ear.

I don't think the queen heard, but she peered at us through her eyeglass. "Are these the princesses from the Academy?" she asked, and she did NOT sound impressed. "Where are my dear twins?"

"The other coaches are just arriving, Your Majesty," Fairy Angora said, and Queen Frizella Marie sailed away to a throne

on a small platform. King Percy
and Lady Whitstable-Kent nodded
kindly at us, and went to sit beside
her. And then, to our HUGE
surprise, we saw Queen Mother
Matilda sweep up and join them.

"Oh NO!" We looked at each other in horror. Was she going to be a judge as well?

A moment later there was a flurry as the rest of the princesses arrived – and we saw the twins.

"WOW!" I could feel my eyes popping. "WOW!"

The twins looked EXACTLY like the funny drawing we'd done of Little Bo Peep! They were wearing pale-green silk hooped dresses with LOADS of frilly petticoats, sun bonnets, crooks tied with bows – and the highest heels you ever saw!

"Whew!" Lindsey whistled. "They must have taken the drawing! Remember? So that's why it disappeared..."

Chapter Five

TAN TARRA TARRA!

A page blew a trumpet, and King Percy stood up.

"Princesses!" he announced. "We would like you to parade before us so we can make our decision. Each group will stop in front of us, and explain why they think their costumes are appropriate for farm work. We will then make our decision, and the winners will be introduced to the little lamb before the Grand Parade begins."

"Do we need the explanations?" Queen Frizella Marie smiled a chilly smile. "I'm quite certain who should win!" And she gave the twins a little wave.

King Percy coughed politely. "Lady Whit and I think we should hear how our princesses have made their decisions. Tulip Room, would you be kind enough to begin?"

We were SO nervous! But we took turns to explain how the

jodhpurs could be washed, and the rubber boots cleaned, and how we could bend and stretch and run. Queen Mother Matilda frowned and Queen Frizella Marie even yawned behind her hand, but King Percy and Lady Whit smiled encouragingly as we finished.

"The Princesses Diamonde and Gruella!" announced the page, and the twins minced out. Both the queens clapped loudly.

The twins curtsied very low, and Diamonde began, "We've chosen green so that the grass stains won't show..."

"OH!" I couldn't help myself –
I gave the loudest gasp. How
COULD they? They hadn't just
copied our drawing, they'd copied
our ideas!

Queen Mother Matilda looked
angrily towards me. "SILENCE!"

She turned to King Percy. "Now, perhaps, you can see just why I suggested Princess Caitlin was removed from this competition!" She shook her finger at me. "One more word, and I shall send you back to the Academy!"

"Let us continue," King Percy said calmly. "Princess Diamonde, you were saying?"

But before Diamonde could say another word there was a massive commotion at the back of the marquee, and a tiny lamb came tearing in, chased by two boys and a red-faced Farmer Kate.

"Baaa!" it bleated. "Baaaa!"

Diamonde began to scream, and Gruella shrieked. They tried to run, but their high heels caught in the carpet, and they tripped and fell over in a flurry of skirts.

The lamb sped past them and headed for the doorway, but when the princesses from Lily Room held out their arms it changed direction and rushed to the side of the marquee. With a wriggle and a twist it squeezed underneath the canvas, but just before it disappeared I saw the little black spots on its back.

I didn't stop to think. I dived after it, calling, "Topper! Topper!"

As I crawled out on the other side I realised it had begun to rain. The grass was soaking, and my clothes got covered in mud as I struggled to my feet. "Topper!"

I called...and then I saw him. He was standing a little way away, looking back at me. "It's all right..." I whispered, and tiptoed towards him. I was nearly there when a trumpet suddenly sounded.

TAN TARRA! TAN TARRA!

Topper leapt in the air – so I flung myself forwards and JUST managed to catch him. He struggled in my arms, but then quietened down as I began to sooth him gently.

"Phew!" I told him. "We'd better get you back." And I carried him round the outside of the marquee, and back inside...

As I walked in there was SUCH a massive burst of cheering and clapping that if I hadn't been holding Topper tightly he'd have run away again!

Chapter Six

"Well DONE, Caitlin!" Fairy G boomed, and King Percy came hurrying towards me, a broad smile on his face. Lady Whit was close behind him, and she was beaming as well.

"Go and stand on the platform, Princess Caitlin!" King Percy told me. "We all want to see how your outfit has survived you crawling through the mud to save a dear little lamb!"

Lady Whit laughed her haw-hawing laugh. "Couldn't have had a better test!"

So I went to stand on the platform, with Topper snuggled in my arms.

"There!" King Percy looked at

the two queens. "I think you have to agree that this is the winning design!"

Both Queen Mother Matilda and Queen Frizella Marie nodded their heads stiffly.

"But that's not FAIR!" Diamonde wailed. "What about US?"

King Percy stroked his chin. "Could YOU chase and rescue a runaway lamb, Diamonde?"

Diamonde tried to get up...but couldn't. It wasn't until the page stepped forward, bowed, and offered his hand that the twins were able to walk away...and they didn't say another word.

"Tulip Room are the winners!" King Percy announced. "And now, let the Grand Parade begin!"

And do you know what? We didn't lead Topper in the Grand Parade – we took turns to carry

him! He slept all the way as we paraded round the Royal County Show, even though everyone was shouting and cheering and waving. He only woke up as the procession ended!

It didn't matter a bit that I was all messy and muddy – in fact, King Percy said it was very suitable!

Farmer Kate was waiting for us. "Time for his bottle," she said, and she let us feed him before she took him back to the farm.

"Come and see him soon," she called as she carried the sleepy little lamb away.

That night we couldn't stop talking about Topper.

"Let's go and see him again tomorrow," Lindsey said at last with a huge yawn.

"That would be brilliant," Abigail agreed.

"Tulip for Topper!" Rebecca suggested, and we all smiled as we snuggled down in our beds, and blew each other kisses...

And it's Tulip for you as well. Why? Because you're our very special friend.

Don't miss **The Tiara Club** website at:

www.tiaraclub.co.uk

Keep up to date with the latest
Tiara Club books and meet all
your favourite princesses!

There is SO much to see and do,
including games and activities. You can
even become an exclusive member of the
Tiara Club Princess Academy.

PLUS, there are exciting
competitions with truly
FABULOUS prizes!

Be a Perfect Princess – check it out today!

What happens next?
Find out in

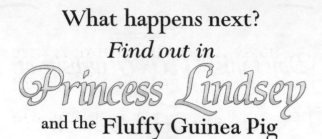

Princess Lindsey
and the Fluffy Guinea Pig

Dear Princess – I'm SO pleased to meet you! I'm Princess Lindsey, and maybe you've already met Mia, Bethany, Caitlin, Abigail and Rebecca? We all share Tulip Room, and we're the very best friends ever. Do you have a pet? There's a fabulous Holiday Home for Pets here at Diamond Turrets, and we all help look after the animals that come to stay – it's SUCH fun...except when the twins cause trouble, of course!

My most favourite animals are guinea pigs – I just LOVE them! Their eyes are just a little bit too close together, which makes them look really sweet, and they make the cutest *wink! wink!* noise.

When I arrived at Diamond Turrets and discovered there was a Holiday Home for Pets as well as the farm and the Safari Park I was SO thrilled. The first thing I asked was, "Are there any guinea pigs staying at the moment?" and I was really disappointed when there weren't. But then, one Thursday, it was Tulip Room's turn to work with the pets – and there was the most DIVINE guinea pig. He was trying to hide himself under a lettuce leaf, but his bottom was sticking out. (That's another of reasons why I love them so much; they're just SO silly.)

"Wow," I breathed. "Where did he come from?"

Lady May, who looks after the Holiday Home, smiled at me. "He belongs to Diamonde and Gruella's aunt, and their cousins. I'm worried about him, though. He arrived yesterday evening, and he hasn't eaten anything."

"Maybe he was upset by the

journey," Abigail suggested.

Lady May looked doubtful. "Most guinea pigs can't resist cucumber, or carrot. But I've tried him with just about everything, and he isn't interested."

"Could I try?" I asked, but before Lady May could answer, Diamonde and Gruella sailed through the door.

"Where's Monty?" Diamonde demanded. "Auntie Emmalina said he was coming to stay here while she's on tour, and WE want to look after him!" And she and Gruella pushed their way in front of us until they were leaning over the top of Monty's cage.

"Hello, Monty," Gruella said loudly. She made a grab at him, but he squeaked wildly and ran behind his water bottle.

∼ Want to read more? ∼
Princess Lindsey and the Fluffy Guinea Pig
is out now!

3 1901 04917 4693